Camping Paradiso

BY JENNY OLDFIELD

ILLUSTRATED BY FRANCIS SCAPPATICCI

"I've lost your father!" Mrs Wayman cried, leaning far out over the ship's rail. The waves frothed miles below. "I can't find him anywhere!"

"He's probably in the bar," Wanda said. Her mother made such a fuss that other passengers were growing nervous. They all stared down into the foaming sea. "Getting drunk," Wanda added loudly. It was a lie but it calmed people down. They went back to their Bistros of Brittany guidebooks, and their First Steps in French for Foreign Foot Travellers. Mrs Wayman scuttled off down the metal stairs. Wanda winked at her friend Flora. They went on counting seagulls: "Five hundred and thirty-three, five hundred and thirty-four ... "

Wanda had a mind like a computer, but twice as fast. She was fantastic with figures, magic at maths. She had worked out the family's journey to the ferry port to the nearest one hundred metres: 160.5 kilometres measured on the map. "Well, blow me!" her dad said, impressed. Besides, she was super-organised. She had made a list of each item in her suitcase: T-shirts – 7, shorts – 5, knickers – 11, and so on. "So I don't lose anything," she said. Flora had just flung everything in higgledy piggledy. "Never mind, I'll organise it for you when we arrive," Wanda promised.

"Five hundred and sixty-seven, five hundred and sixty-eight ... " They stood on the rail, gazing far out across the English Channel with the salt wind in their faces. They could be explorers like Sir Francis Drake discovering the new world. They could be pirates!

"Wanda, where's your father? Have you seen your dad?" Mrs Wayman's voice came drifting back into their dreams.

"Not in the bar?" Wanda said, still staring at the horizon but sounding surprised. "Try the duty free shop. I saw him in there a while ago."

For the whole of the crossing she sent her worried mum all over the ferry, in and out of bars and restaurants, into the cinema, up to the sun lounge deck, down to the cabins. Meanwhile, Wanda and Flora were Francis and Drake – twin explorers in eye patches and spotted headscarves, discovering Atlanticana and all the gold and diamonds in the universe.

For Wanda had a mind full of fairy tales, but twice as fantastic. Adventure was in her blood. She was sure her great-great-grandparents must have been wizards and witches with wondrous powers. Forget her dreamy dad and worrying mum, Wanda was a throwback to Wisewoman Wayman, head of the tribe and chief storyteller.

"Land ahoy!" Flora squeaked. She leaned further out over the rail and pointed.

"Where?" Wanda said, annoyed. She wanted to be the first to spot it.

"There!"

"Hm." She had to admit Flora was right. "Anyway, all car deck B passengers to assembly point seven!" she barked, before it had time to come up on the loudspeaker.

The other passengers followed the girls to the queue by the inquiry desk, where Wanda and Flora stood and waited patiently with their little rucksacks full of suncream – 1 bottle, sunglasses – 1 pair, reading books – 2, packets of salt 'n vinegar flavour crisps – 3.

"I seem to have lost your mother!" Mr Wayman strolled up at last. His hands were stuffed in his fawn trouser pockets, his hair was a mess. He'd spilt tea down the front of his new white polo shirt. "I can't find her anywhere."

Wanda advised him to stay put with them until Mrs Wayman turned up. "It's only 15.00 hours, and we don't disembark until 15.35. Plenty of time," Wanda said briskly. He nodded and waited with them in the queue.

"What's 'disembark'?" Flora whispered.

"To get off the ship," Wanda explained. She told Flora she would need to get her passport ready. "It's 87 kilometres to the campsite. That's roughly two hours by car, two and a half to allow for my dad getting lost. That means we'll be there at 18.05!"

The two girls beamed like lighthouses. 'Camping Paradiso: swimming pool with giant waterslide, table tennis, boating on the lake, a tent with a fridge and three bedrooms. Two hundred metres from the beach!'

"There you all are!" Mrs Wayman turned up at last, looking exhausted. "I've been looking for you all over the place!" Now she needed something else to worry about. "Are you sure our car is on car deck B, Colin? Did

6

you write it down? They all look the same to me! Are you sure we're in the right queue?"

Meanwhile, Wanda and Flora were cavers exploring giant stalactites as they shuffled down into the dark belly of the ship. "Watch out for falling rocks!" Wanda hissed, squeezing between a Volvo and a Peugeot. They got out their torches, stooped into the back seat, crouched there and waited with held breath for the great rumbling to stop.

"Which way now?" Mr Wayman asked, rolling down the ramp into broad daylight. Men in orange jackets waved them on.

"Turn right, drive on the right, follow signs for the E46 to Bayeux," Wanda told him.

"Welcome to the Campsite Paradiso,
Such a lovely place ... "

Mr Wayman sang at the top of his voice to the tune of an old song. He swerved to avoid a man in a beret on a bicycle.

"Colin!" Mrs Wayman squealed. If a mouse could talk, it would sound like Mrs Wayman.

"Don't worry," Wanda told Flora, "you'll get used to it."

"Welcome to the Campsite Paradiso,
Such a lovely place ... "

they all sang into the French countryside, between miles of yellow sunflowers, along dead straight roads into the evening sun.

CHAPTER 2

The Campsite not-so-Paradiso, as it turned out. The swimming pool with giant waterslide was closed for cleaning. You had to pay ten francs for a game of table tennis. Their tent was covered in giant horseflies, and the beach was nowhere to be seen.

"Still," said Mr Wayman, who was easily pleased, "at least it's sunny." He heaved the cases off the roof-rack.

"Be careful, Colin, that handle's ... loose!" A suitcase broke free and skidded into next door's tent. Mrs Wayman whimpered.

Wanda and Flora shot after it, straight under the awning and into a boy of about their own age who was catching insects in his fishing net. Flora grabbed their case. "Hello, I'm Wanda. Where's the beach please?" Wanda said all in one breath.

"Would you like to see my stick insects?" the boy asked. He held up a see-through plastic sandwich box containing three blades of grass and two sad-looking sticks that moved.

"Ah, poor things!" Flora said. She was more soft hearted than Wanda.

"Where's the beach?" Wanda demanded, hands on hips. Really, it was a very simple question.

The boy lay flat on his stomach to lift the ground sheet. "There's a nest of them somewhere under here," he said.

"Stick insects don't have nests. Where's the beach?!" Wanda screamed.

"Past the pool, through the trees, across the main road, turn left for half a kilometre, turn right, then left again, past the geese, down a lane, past a farm, turn right and you're there," the boy reeled off.

"B-b-but!"

He sighed. "I know. They lied."

"B-b-brochures don't lie!" she protested.

He raised an eyebrow, got up on to his knees and looked pityingly at Wanda. "You're new here. Just you wait."

"Hello. I'm Flora." Flora stepped in because Wanda looked as if she would explode. Flora flashed the boy a bright smile.

"I'm Jim," he said, blushing. He suddenly lost interest in his stick insect collection. He stood up and fiddled with the tent flap. "I could show you the beach," he offered.

"Oh yes please!" Flora gushed.

Traitor! Wanda could have stabbed her to the heart. She glared instead. This Jim boy helped Flora drag their suitcase back to the tent, went for his towel and was back again before you could draw breath, with his short blond haircut, his multi-coloured Bermuda shorts, his trainers and his suntan.

"Mum, can we go to the beach, please!" Wanda whined. She knew the answer would be no, it was too late, they hadn't eaten, they might get lost, etcetera.

Then Jim would have to go and get lost too.

"Yes, all right," her mum said.

"Good idea," her dad agreed.

Wanda could have cried. Flora beamed. They headed for the setting sun while Mr and Mrs Miller, Jim's mum and dad, made friends with Wanda's mum and dad over a bottle of red wine.

"There's the showers, there's the bar, there's the shop, there's the games room," Jim rattled off. "And there," he said, pointing to a man in very tight jeans, with a blue and white striped T-shirt covering a round belly, "is Monsieur Bourgeois!"

The man was snatching a ping-pong ball in the middle of a game. He was ordering everyone out. He was locking up the games room and clearing the volleyball pitch. Children sloped off in dismay.

"Who's he?" Flora frowned.

"The manager of the camp." Jim headed off through some pine trees. "Public enemy number one!"

Glancing back at Monsieur Bourgeois' neat little black moustache and great key ring, Wanda got the sniff of an adventure.

Jim led them on, tracking like hunters through the forest. It was late. The beach was almost empty when they arrived. They were desert nomads trekking across the wastes of the Sahara. They swam. They were scuba divers searching off the coast of Spain for shipwrecks. They trailed back, salty-skinned, to Camping Paradiso. Now they were three children too tired even to eat.

"Good job," Jim said. "Bourgeois closes the pizza and french fries shop at seven o'clock."

"No hot water again!" Jim's dad grumbled, fresh from the shower.

"The calor gas has run out." Jim's mum stood and sighed over the dead cooker. "Again."

"Dratted flies," Mr Wayman said, failing to swat a few.

"Colin, do you think we should risk drinking this tap water? Are you sure it's all right?" Mrs Wayman asked, peering suspiciously into a jug full of it. She hadn't noticed the flies yet.

The girls quickly snuggled into their sleeping-bags. They lay there listening to the traffic. After a while, Flora whispered in a tiny voice, "Wanda, what do you think of Jim?"

Wanda didn't answer. She closed her eyes and pretended to be asleep. "Happy holiday!" she thought.

CHAPTER 3

Next morning before the cock crew, Mrs Wayman's scream woke the whole campsite. "C-C-Colin, don't move!" she cried. But it was too late.

The canvas inner tent shook and shuddered. Mr Wayman had leapt out of his sleeping-bag and careered after something. He was trying to thump it with his trainer. Mrs Wayman squealed and squealed.

Inside their own little sleeping compartments Flora and Wanda groaned. They'd have to get up. It wasn't even light as they struggled into their shorts and T-shirts, and came out armed with their own trainers. "What is it, Dad?" Wanda wanted to know. "What's wrong?"

In the half-light her father seemed to be conducting an invisible orchestra with his shoe. He waved his arms in the air, ducking and diving, while her mother cowered in a corner whimpering.

"Drat!" her dad said, swiping the roof.

"It's a horsefly," Wanda told a sleepy Flora, pointing to a dozy insect which circled over the cooker. "Sort of. Look. But they don't bite, according to that Jim boy, and I can't see what all the fuss is about." She unzipped the outer tent to let the dazed fly reach safety.

"Has it gone?" her mum whimpered. She still had her hands over her face. "I woke up for some reason, I don't know what, and there it was squatting there on your nose, Colin, just staring at me! I opened my eyes and there it was! Ugh!"

"There, it's gone now. Wanda shooed it off." He went to comfort her.

Wanda beckoned Flora over to the tent flap and pointed secretly to the green and blue outer shell. She raised her finger to her mouth. "Ssh!" There in the grey dawn they counted the great black clots clinging to the tent, each nearly three centimetres long, each waking up to a new day and drying the dew off their coarse wings. "Sixty-three, sixty-four, sixty-five … ," Wanda whispered. Now she knew why these things were called flysheets.

"Don't tell your mum!" Flora giggled.

Wanda looked up. "They're dropping down from that tree, look!" They fell silently from an unusual, scaly pine tree.

"There's millions of them!"

"Not millions," Wanda said scornfully. "Just a few hundred."

"They'll drive your mum crazy!"

"I think we'd better ask to move tents. If they're up in that funny tree and this is the only one of them on the site, this must be the only tent that's bothered by them. Come on, let's have a shower and go and find this Mister Bourgeois. He'll have to put us in another tent!"

With a perfect sense of logic Wanda marched off to the shower block with her towel. Flora followed more slowly. She didn't mind moving tents, only it meant they wouldn't be next door to Jim. It was a big campsite. They might be put way over the other side by the lake. It was a pity. She looked lingeringly at Jim's zipped up tent as they tramped over the dewy grass. Wanda had the same thought in mind as she led the way, but she on the other hand felt very cheerful. No more boys in their gruesome swimming shorts. She sang in the shower. She would tell this Mister Bourgeois the flies were a health hazard. He'd have to move them before breakfast, before the flies got active. By the time they were crunching their croissants they would have no flies, a new view and new neighbours.

"Non!" Monsieur Bourgeois crossed his arms and frowned down at them.

"No? What do you mean, no?" Wanda cried. "It's dirty! It's disgusting! Those flies are this big!" She exaggerated with her outstretched thumb and forefinger.

"Non!" he repeated. "Ees not possible!"

"But there are loads of empty tents!" Wanda protested. "Over there by the lake. There are dozens!"

He shook his head. "Full. No possible! Go away, leetle girl!" He turned to his computer screen and ignored them.

"B-but!" Wanda spluttered.

Flora had the sense to grab her arm and drag her out of the office. "Never mind, maybe the flies will all go away as soon as the sun comes up properly." She gave Jim a cheerful wave as he trotted by with a long stick of French bread under his arm. "Come on, let's see if your mum's recovered."

They went back to the tent. By now the flies were crawling all over the roof, saying good morning. Mrs Wayman was sitting petrified in the car with all the windows closed. Mr Wayman, still unshaven but heroic, was swatting in vain.

"Here," he said, handing Wanda a fifty-franc note, "buy some bread from the shop, and while you're at it see if they sell flyspray."

"What's French for flyspray?" Wanda asked sulkily. Flora was already sitting at next door's table with Jim, planning a go on the waterslide.

Wanda's dad gave her a dirty look. "Just go," he said.

So Wanda went and bought the croissants – and something she picked up off a shelf called Zapp. It was in a green can and had a drawing of a dead fly on it. The horrible Monsieur Bourgeois took her fifty francs and refused to give her any change. "Ees very expensive," he sniffed, rapping the aerosol on the counter. "Now, go away!"

Mumbling, she trailed back. Bourgeois was mean, he was a cheat, and he told lies. And he did it all in a French accent, so she was helpless. She sat outside the tent in the open air, chewing her crusty bread, sipping very milky coffee. The flies cavorted on the tent in the sunshine. "I'm gonna have to do something about that man!" Wanda said. She set her super-brain to work on the problem.

CHAPTER 4

You cannot always come up with a miracle, even if you are Wanda Wonderwoman Wayman. Not when there's boating on the lake, playing crazy golf, or giant waterslides to divert your attention.

"The slide's just opened!" Flora flew across to the tent to wriggle into her swimming costume.

Wanda knew it because she could hear the first squeals and yells and splashes from there. The top of the slide peeked above the tallest trees. There were kids up there on the platform, queuing to launch themselves down the curling blue plastic snake.

"Come on, Wanda!" Flora yelled.

Wanda gave in. She abandoned the Battle of Bourgeois masterplan and rushed in for her swimsuit. She was ready at the same time as her friend. "Jim says you have to pay ten francs for ten tokens. You get a kind of bracelet of them from the office. He's going to show us," Flora explained.

"I'll bet he is," Wanda muttered, deliberately lagging behind. They bought their tokens and headed by the side of the pool to the great metal staircase. By then, sheer excitement had overtaken her.

"Women and children first!" a tense voice inside her head ordered. "Man the lifeboats!" They were escaping from the hold of a sinking cruise ship, the 'Titanic'.

Every second counted, up the metal stairs, scrambling to safety. They reached the top. "Go ahead, women and children first!" The icy water swirled miles below. The ship tilted at a crazy angle. Wanda clung to the rails. She gritted her teeth, steeled herself. Then she flung herself through the opening of the waterslide head first. She shot forward, streamlining her body, following the curves and using the angles. She gathered more speed. Water sprayed with great force in her face and down every crevice of her swimsuit as the blue chute straightened out. There was the aquamarine of the pool, there were Jim and Flora waist deep, screeching as she plummeted. She hit the water, dived under, came up with her hair plastered to her face, spluttering and whooping. The boy behind crashed into the water after her. Wanda caught her breath and started grinning all over her face.

"Again?" Jim asked, halfway out of the pool.

Flora hesitated. "Maybe we should save our tokens?"

Wanda laughed and hauled herself out of the water. "Again!" she cried. She was first up the metal steps, two at a time, handing over the token and launching herself feet first, then sideways, then in a two with Flora, then three at a time with Jim, squealing and gasping until the tokens ran out.

She didn't even pause for breath. "We need more thingummybobs!" Wanda yelled. "Come on!" The waterslide was the best thing on the site. She'd already worked out that if she spent every franc of her pocket money on it, she'd have two hundred and eighty goes. That worked out at forty a day. She never did anything by halves.

She dripped into the tent, swatted flies off her rucksack and dived in for more money.

"Don't spend it all at once!" her mum warned from the safety of her fly-free zone inside the car.

"I will!" Wanda promised. "Ready?" she asked Flora and Jim with a grin.

They took a short cut over the crazy golf course to the office for more tokens, only to find a small queue, and Mr Bourgeois behind the desk arguing with an elderly couple. The children stood there and dripped impatiently while the argument developed.

"Non! Non! Non!" Monsieur Bourgeois was yelling. This much they understood. He was waving his arms, and the old pair were pointing at a piece of paper. Bourgeois kept repeating a number and writing it down. The old man was shaking his head. From the sign language they could tell that Bourgeois was charging them much more than they wanted to pay.

"Excuse me, are you English?" A young woman with a blonde ponytail had come out from an inner office. She spoke with an accent, but clearly and precisely.

"American." The old man looked relieved.

"And you don't speak French? Wait a moment, please." She turned and discussed the problem with Bourgeois. "Monsieur Bourgeois says this is high season, this is the most expensive time." She shook her head apologetically. She was pretty and tanned, with light grey eyes. "I'm very sorry. You must pay the top amount."

"But we came six weeks ago. We fixed a cheap rate because we planned to stay so long!" The old man refused to give in. "We made a deal here. We don't have a large budget, as a matter of fact!" His wife was nearly in tears.

Bourgeois pushed the blonde girl aside. He lifted the desk top and stood face to face with the old couple. "Give me my money!" he shouted. His English was suddenly much better. "Or I will telephone to the police. Understand?"

"I'll give it to him," the old lady said with a sigh. She fished more notes out of her purse. "We don't want to make any trouble."

Bourgeois grabbed the notes. He stuck them in his jeans pocket and began propelling the old folks towards the glass doors. "And now go! Don't come back. Never again, go!"

"Now just one heck of a minute!" the old man protested. But it was useless. Everyone in the office watched in embarrassment as they were hustled down the path and into their cream van. Peroline, the blonde French girl, was red with anger and shame as she stayed inside to deal with the crazy golf tickets and waterslide tokens.

She took Wanda's ten francs and met her eye to eye. "Yes, I know," she sighed. She handed Wanda her tokens. "But he's the boss and what can I do?" She shook her head hopelessly.

Somehow it spoiled the next few rides on the slide, thinking of that old lady in tears and Bourgeois' black, bristling moustache spitting rude words at their disappearing van.

"What's up?" Jim asked. They were leaning on the bar while he bought ice lollies all round. "You feeling sick or something?"

"Sick of Bourgeois," Wanda said, biting the nose cone off her spaceship lolly.

"Want to get him back?" Jim asked. He flicked his own lollipop stick into a bin.

Wanda, who sulked when other people had good ideas, was about to say no. But she recalled Jim's skill with the fishing net, and his interest in insect life. Suddenly she had a bright idea. "Yes!" she said, looking Jim full in the freckled face. "As a matter of fact I do!"

CHAPTER 5

There were times, Wanda knew, when you had to make friends with those who could be useful. True, it was hard. She had to swallow all her scorn for Jim and his multi-coloured swimming shorts. She had to pretend that she didn't mind boys in general and know-all boys in particular. She had to put up with Flora's soppy smile of gratitude. "This is what we're gonna do!" she said. The three of them put their heads together.

"Capture ... secret ... wait until morning ... surprise!" they giggled.

They were French resistance fighters in the Second World War. They would crawl in the undergrowth on their bellies before dawn and take the enemy by surprise. They would grit their teeth and never give in to torture. They would take their secret to the grave.

"What are you three up to?" Mr Wayman chuckled. He had brought his video camera to the poolside to film them on the waterslide. "No good as usual, I expect."

Wanda eyed him coolly. "Actually, Dad, we're just discussing ideas for tonight's disco," she lied.

"Disco!" This didn't fit Mr Wayman's view of his brainbox, tomboy daughter. "Dancing!"

"Yes!" She looked him in the eye.

"Whereabouts?"

"At the bar," Jim said. "Every night. Tonight's a fancy dress one. Are you coming?"

Mr Wayman looked more and more startled. Wanda was definitely up to something. "Fancy dress?"

"You can dress in anything to do with the sea," Jim explained. "A sailor or an octopus or something like that."

"I'll have to check with your mother," Mr Wayman said dubiously. He went off shaking his head, forgetting about the filming.

" ... Spy on the enemy ... follow all his movements ... forward planning ... " Wanda, Flora and Jim put their heads together again and thought out every move.

Wanda went to the disco as a mermaid, with a plastic bin-bag around her legs for a tail. This was a clever move which meant she didn't have to dance. She wore a string of giant oyster shells around her neck and a green crêpe-paper wig, waist length. Flora and Jim went as French sailors in blue and white striped T-shirts, like a couple of dozen other kids and Peroline's helper, Pierre.

Peroline ran the disco. She was dressed as an American film star in heart-shaped sunglasses, a strapless top and tight white trousers. She said she was a guest on a cruise ship, and that was to do with the sea, *'n'est ce pas?'* She led the kids in crazy crocodiles across the dance floor, through the bar and out by the pool. Red and blue lights flashed, music crashed. Pierre stood by the sound deck turning up the volume. His eyes followed Peroline everywhere. Wanda was the only one who kept her wits about her as the other kids writhed and yelled to the music. Her legs sweating inside her plastic bag, she scanned the dark corners for Bourgeois.

There he was, overcharging people at the bar as usual. Wanda's eyes narrowed. She watched as he slipped change into his pocket and rang up four prices on the till when he had only served three drinks. She saw her own father pay what amounted to £3.50 for a small glass of lager. Wanda did the quick conversion sum in her head. "We must stop thees man!" she said to herself. She was taking the resistance role seriously. "Zut alors!" It was the only French swear word she could recall from the phrase book. ('Zut alors!' *zyt.* exclamation – dash it, good heavens, etc.)

Bourgeois wore a fixed grin above his Breton T-shirt. "Just you wait until tomorrow morning!" Wanda said to herself. She despaired of Flora and Jim being able to do anything useful this evening. There they were in the middle of the dance floor, gyrating to the music: "We are sailing! We are sailing, cross the blah blah ... "

Then it was the end, the lights died, Pierre pulled the switches on the sound deck and Peroline made sure all the kids got back to the right parents. Bourgeois snapped the shutter down on the bar and began herding everyone out, quick march!

"Did you bring the torch, Colin?" Mrs Wayman whimpered, out on the terrace. "I can't see a thing!"

"Yes, here." The thin beam lit up the grass. Mr Wayman turned and said a cheery "Great evening!" to an unresponsive Bourgeois.

Wanda peeled off her fish's tail. She heard Peroline come up to monster-manager and speak politely.

Bourgeois tutted, put both hands into his tight trouser pockets and shook his head. Peroline, her blonde hair fluttering in the night breeze, put her hands on her hips. Another argument! Wanda was all ears.

"What's she saying?" she asked the adoring Pierre.

Pierre put a finger to his lips. " 'e will not pay 'er the money for running the disco!" he warned.

"Of all the mean ... !"

"Ssh!" Pierre stood poised like a tennis player about to argue with a linesman's call; tall and tanned, with a beautiful haircut.

Peroline and Bourgeois battled it out. Finally, the manager shouted a short sentence, turned and stormed off.

Pierre ran after him, gestured, shouted back. But the judge's decision was final. Pierre came back to the terrace and put his arm round Peroline's shoulder. Wanda's curiosity was killing her. "What's he done? What did he say?" she asked.

"The pig, 'e refused to pay! 'E 'as given 'er the sack!" Pierre explained. He gave a very French shrug and went on comforting his girlfriend. "When I complained, Monsieur Bourgeois, 'e says, 'Tell that to the supervisor tomorrow!' Then 'e walks away! No money. No job!"

"Tomorrow? The supervisor?" Wanda tried to think straight. This could make their plan work perfectly! But even she was moved by the touching scene of Pierre gently holding a distressed Peroline in his arms in the moonlight by the shimmering pool. Silhouetted trees rustled in the breeze as Peroline sobbed. Wanda's skin tingled and she felt herself going to pieces. Her bottom lip began to wobble.

"Wanda!" Mrs Wayman's voice piped through the darkness. "Where is she? Colin, I think she's been kidnapped!"

"Here!" Wanda said, coming down to earth. She ran after her mum and dad. She told Flora and Jim the latest news about Peroline. They shook their heads, open-mouthed. "It means our secret operation has *got* to work!" Wanda reminded them. "Reassemble outside our tent at 0600 hours, okay!"

The others nodded, pale faced in the moonlight.

"That man must be stopped!" she thought as they dived for their sleeping-bags. "He must be stopped, for everyone's sake!"

CHAPTER 6

Operation Horsefly began in the grey light of dawn. The grass was wet with dew and a convenient sea mist cloaked the tents of the Campsite Paradiso. Wanda crawled out of her sleeping-bag, ready dressed in jumper and shorts. She collected Flora, unzipped the tent, and met up with Jim on the deserted grass between their emplacements.

It was cold and damp and deserted. Zipped tents stretched row after row. You could have had a twenty minute shower in the shower block without a queue of a dozen people shouting insults at you in at least four different languages. You could have played crazy golf without anyone laughing. But they had more important things to do.

"Got the fishing net?" Wanda asked.

Jim nodded, clenching his teeth to stop them from chattering.

Wanda turned to Flora. "Remember the food box?"

Flora held it up proudly in both hands.

"Good! Now all we have to do is wait for them to drop!"

They all looked up anxiously at the strange pine tree above the Waymans' tent. All seemed peaceful. The tent itself was grubby with sap, but clear of its uninvited wildlife. So Wanda, Flora and Jim each took a white plastic chair and positioned themselves to one side, patiently waiting.

Then the sun came up – a ball of golden fire through the branches of the pine tree. Birds sang like crazy in other trees. The whole sky went pink and the mist vanished like magic. Still no one stirred. "Soon!" Wanda whispered. They stared up at the tree in silence.

Then one by one the giant flies dropped. Like silent ink blots they appeared on the green flysheet, ruffling their wings, crawling slowly towards another sunlit day. "Now!" Wanda mouthed, pointing to their first victim.

Jim leapt forward with his net, Flora at his heels. Swiftly he brought the net down over a fly. In vain it struggled as expertly he flicked his wrist and scooped the fly into Flora's outstretched box. She snapped the lid closed on the fly before it had time to come to its senses. "One!" Wanda counted, with a thumbs up. She pointed again. Jim scooped, Flora lidded. "Two! Three! Four! ... Twenty-one!"

"Jim?" a voice said at last from inside next door's tent. The sun cast a warm pink glow along the avenue of tents. There was a great unzipping, then Mrs Miller's tousled red head appeared. Jim whistled his net overhead, miming an elaborate butterfly chase. Flora whipped the twenty-one horseflies behind her back. Wanda said a casual good morning. "You're up early," Mrs Miller said suspiciously.

"Certainly," Wanda said. "We lepidopterists always catch the worm, you know. Like early birds!"

"What?" Jim's mum handed him a water container to fill. "Don't talk silly. Butterflies don't come out this early, you should know that, Jimmy!"

"Don't call me Jimmy!" he hissed, resisting her affectionate pat.

She laughed and challenged him to show her his early morning species. Then she disappeared inside to start brewing tea.

"Phew!" Flora said. The flies buzzed furiously inside the box.

"Have we got enough?" Jim asked.

Wanda was stabbing airholes into the lid with a kebab skewer. Then she stuck some blades of grass down the holes. The clear plastic gave a good view of twenty-one crawling, fat, black, disgusting flies. "Easily!" she said with grim satisfaction, just as her mum ventured out in her flowered dressing-gown and worried face.

"Colin!" Mrs Wayman whispered in surprise. "Come out here and look a minute!" She peered nervously at the flysheet.

"What is it?" Wanda's dad emerged, fish-slice at the ready. These days he swatted automatically in his sleep.

"No, no, there's no need. Look, Colin!" Mrs Wayman sounded as if the Red Sea had parted. "Look, not a single fly! It's a miracle!" She breathed her first sigh of relief of the entire holiday, and went back inside for her bath towel and toilet bag.

"Well!" Mr Wayman said, mystified.

The children grinned innocently. "I should keep the fish-slice ready, Dad, just in case," Wanda warned, prophetically.

For just as her mum emerged, another fly dropped.

It made the mistake of landing on the pretty mauve and yellow flowers of her dressing-gown. She felt it thud. She opened her mouth and screamed. Mr Wayman swatted furiously.

The whole site woke with a chorus of zips, coughs, dogs barking, kids crying. Mrs Wayman shot off to the shower to scrub herself all over, while Wanda, Flora and Jim quietly tended their angry prisoners in the long grass at the back of the tent.

CHAPTER 7

After that they all had different jobs to attend to. Flora went to the office to hang round innocently until she could discover what time the supervisor was due to arrive. Bourgeois was there, bristling and hustling money out of people as usual. Pierre was there to hand out waterslide tokens, but Peroline wasn't. He raised his handsome, dark eyebrows at innocent, smiling Flora. "At least later I shall have some peace," he sighed. "When le patron meets with the supervisor."

"Le patron?" Flora played really dumb.

"Monsieur Bourgeois. He has a meeting at midday."

Flora's face lit up. "Thanks!" she said, and shot off.

"For what?" Pierre said to thin air, with one of his shrugs.

Jim, the insect expert, had to guard the prisoners. Every time a new squeal from inside the Wayman car signified the arrival of a new horsefly on top of their tent, he was tempted to rush out with his net. But Wanda's orders were to stay put, keep guard, feed the hostages when necessary. Wanda had a way of making things crystal clear. So Jim stayed by the box, comparing the boring horsefly with the fascinating stick insect. Flora's bright smile kept creeping into his thoughts. He smiled at the

39

memory. He found it was a good way of passing the time during guard duty.

Wanda, the brainbox, Wanda the wonderkid, put pen to paper.

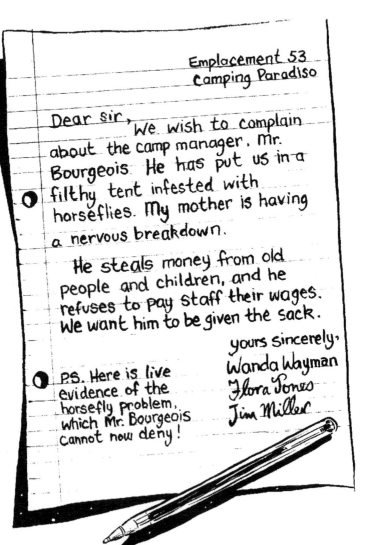

Emplacement 53
Camping Paradiso

Dear sir, We wish to complain about the camp manager. Mr. Bourgeois. He has put us in a filthy tent infested with horseflies. My mother is having a nervous breakdown.

He steals money from old people and children, and he refuses to pay staff their wages. We want him to be given the sack.

yours sincerely,
Wanda Wayman
Flora Jones
Jim Miller

P.S. Here is live evidence of the horsefly problem, which Mr. Bourgeois cannot now deny!

She wondered about squashing a specimen and sticking it with Blutak to the foot of the letter. She would label it 'Dead evidence'. But she decided that twenty-one live ones in the box would do nicely. So she sealed the letter. It was ten o'clock, time to change the guard. The plan was running like a well-oiled machine. Only two hours to go before they swept from the tent like invading Arab horsemen, down to the office on a unsuspecting Bourgeois!

It was 12.02. The flies were buzzing loudly in their box as they marched single file past the shop, down three steps, past the games room to the office. Jim opened the door for the girls: Wanda with her clean white envelope, Flora with the buzzing box. Pierre greeted them with a sad smile.

"Hi. We would like to see Mr Bourgeois!" Wanda announced.

Pierre looked cautiously at all three of them. "'Ello, what is this noise?" he asked. He looked under the desk, up at the window, behind the magazine rack to try and track it down.

"What noise?" they chorused, looking as though butter wouldn't melt. "Is Mr Bourgeois busy in his office, please?" Wanda pointed to the back room.

"No. What is this buzz-buzz-buzzing?" Pierre had reached for the flyspray, but still couldn't spot the culprits. He sprayed the empty air. "He has gone to meet with the supervisor at the main gate, I think. Then he will bring 'er back here."

"Her?" Wanda queried.

"Yes, the supervisor, Mademoiselle Popigneau."

"We'll wait," Wanda said with grim determination.

"Outside?" Flora suggested. The flies were behaving really badly in the box behind her back.

So they went out and sat on the grass. All should soon be well. The supervisor would come, Wanda would give her the letter of complaint, Flora would present the evidence, then goodbye Mr Bourgeois!

"It's her!" Jim spotted them first. A woman was coming down the drive with the pot-bellied manager.

"Can't be!" Flora gasped.

The woman was tall and slender with silky black hair. There wasn't a single crease on her apple-green suit, or a hair out of place. She glided down the path like a shampoo advert, smiling to left and right.

"It is!" Wanda exclaimed. The woman carried a natty blue briefcase to match her high-heeled shoes. Green and blue were the campsite colours. Wanda jumped up to meet her, waving the vital letter. "Excuse me!"

Bourgeois had spotted the three troublemakers and reacted quick as a flash. "Ah, the leetle children!" 'Leetle' rhymed with 'beetle', and his oily smile beamed down on them. "And 'ow are you liking the Camping Paradiso, eh?" He snatched Wanda's letter with a false "aha!". He turned to his boss. "English. Such nice, pretty children!" He turned back to Wanda. "I will put this letter in the post to England for you, okay?" Then he was whisking past them into the office with the supermodel.

"Hey, we want to … !" Wanda jumped in front of them, barring the door.

"Tut-tt-tt-tt! The manners!" Bourgeois wagged a finger. The supervisor-supermodel smiled and turned her untroubled, tanned face to the sun.

"But we want to ... !" Wanda, seeing her scrunched-up letter disappear into Bourgeois' back pocket, grabbed the evidence from Flora. This would soon wipe the smile off his face. The flies roared inside their box.

"Ugh!" The woman looked down and her bright red lips pursed in horror. The fat flies buzzed and bashed the sides of the transparent box. She stepped smartly back.

"But this is disgusting!" Bourgeois stepped in again and grabbed the box, pushing Wanda off balance. "This is cruel!" They couldn't believe it – he became a Friend of the Earth and opened the box! He carefully released every single piece of evidence.

Dazed at first, the insects crawled on to the grass. They felt the fresh air, shook their wings and soared. Twenty-one carefully collected witnesses to bad management! He beamed up at them. The supervisor nodded her approval.

Flora, Jim and Wanda stared in horror. "That was our evidence!" Flora whimpered.

"And now," Bourgeois clapped his hands, ignoring them completely, "lunch!" He held open the door for his glamorous boss. "And for the leetle children ... " He paused, went to the counter with his sickly smile, and handed each of them a bracelet of waterslide tokens. "This is free, a gift from me, le patron!" he said with an oily laugh.

Pierre stood there flabbergasted. Wanda was speechless.

The supervisor nodded. "How kind! Be good!" she said to them in her husky voice. Then she disappeared into the inner office. Bourgeois smiled and smiled. The door closed.

"Wow!" Jim and Flora said, jangling the tokens.

Only Wanda felt things hadn't gone quite according to plan. An empty box and ten tokens each was all they had to show for their careful campaign.

"Eh bien!" Bourgeois burst out of his private office before they had time to recover. No supervisor, no smile. He made a blowing sound with his lips and ripped Wanda's letter to shreds in front of their eyes. He grabbed back the plastic tokens and gave each child a smart tap on the back of the head instead; snatch - biff, snatch-pat, snatch-smack! Ouch! Ouch! Ouch!

He glared down at them then turned to Pierre with new instructions. "No more rides on the slide for these three!" he hissed. "Not today. Not tomorrow. Never, you hear? Never no more!"

He stared at them one last time, then returned to his supervisor, to be charming as ever over wine and Camembert.

CHAPTER 8

It is hard to enjoy your holiday when you are banned from the best thing on the site. Jim wore a 'not fair' face all afternoon as the yells and screams from the giant waterslide echoed everywhere. He went off with Flora to boat on the lake, as far away as possible.

Wanda stayed put by the tent, trying to read. But the pages were too white and the print darted about like ants in the fierce sunlight.

"I'll tell you what," Mr Wayman said in passing, looking anxiously across at Wanda's mother, "your mum's going a nice shade of lobster inside that car. She won't even open the window!"

"Tell that to the patron!" Wanda said darkly. She was watching Bourgeois on his afternoon tour of the site, perched on a poor little moped. He went up and down the rows of tents, black moustache bristling, sitting bolt upright.

"Maybe I will!" Wanda's dad said, stepping right in front of the bike. Bourgeois stuck his legs straight out to the side and stopped. "I demand to be moved to a fly-free zone!" Mr Wayman said in a loud voice, waving his arms around. Bourgeois gave him a stony stare. "Look at this! Look!" Mr Wayman flapped his arms across the flysheet. A swarm of giant flies rose, then settled.

Bourgeois shrugged. He opened the canvas bag which was strapped across his shoulder, took out a can and squirted it in the direction of the flysheet. The flies just looked and laughed.

"That's no earthly good!" Mr Wayman said. "We want to be moved. We demand to be moved! My wife's slowly microwaving to death inside that car, look!"

Nothing would shake Bourgeois. He spread his hands in a gesture of refusal. "Not possible," he said. He revved his moped and lurched off along the path, immune to poor Mrs Wayman's blotchy pink face and to Mr Wayman's crumpled anger.

"You're wasting your time, Dad," Wanda said, examining the marks made by the plastic seat on the back of her legs. "I already tried!" She said no more. She grabbed a towel and headed for the beach, where she would have time to sit and think.

The sun was low over the sea when Wanda arrived, and the tide was far out. Families were packing up their picnic boxes and beach umbrellas, ready to go home. A few couples walked hand in hand at the water's edge.

It was only now, after the failure of Operation Horsefly, that Wanda realised what they were up against. Bourgeois was ruining people's holidays right, left and centre, with no one to stop him. The supervisor was too busy painting her fingernails and conditioning her hair to bother with unpleasant little things like complaints.

The poor old tourists came off worst. Her mum had spent forty-eight hours inside a boiling hot car, for goodness sake! Bossy Bourgeois was turning Camping Paradiso into a camping disaster!

Deep in thought, Wanda kicked up hot, dry sand, too busy thinking to notice that she had walked slap bang into the middle of a little knot of people.

It was only the bright silver and gold juggling clubs whirling in the air which brought her out of her daydream. They flew up into the blue sky, twirled in an arc, fell and were caught with a thud by ... Peroline!

"Aah! Ooh!" the crowd gasped, clapping and dropping francs and centimes into her upturned beach hat. Peroline stood, legs braced, flipping the clubs expertly in the air. They glinted and sparkled and landed with safe regularity in her hands. They moved like magic.

Wanda was impressed. The crowd clapped one last time as Peroline landed the final club and began to pack them away in a little black suitcase. Then she collected the coins from the hat, tipping them into a silver wallet which she wore on her belt. The audience went off smiling towards their cars. "Very good!" Wanda said, clapping loudest of all. "Very, very good!"

Peroline flicked back her blonde hair. "Thank you. Ah!" She recognised Wanda from the campsite. "How is Camping Paradiso?"

"Not!" Wanda said, turning down the corners of her mouth.

"Not what?"

"Not paradiso. Quite the opposite, in fact."

"I agree," Peroline said with a sad, little laugh. She sat on her closed suitcase, digging her bare toes in the sand. "This is why I must jergle for the money."

"Jergle?" Wanda asked, puzzled.

Peroline mimed throwing up the clubs.

"Oh you mean juggle!" Wanda's mouth spread in a huge grin.

"Yes, jergle," Peroline insisted.

"You mean you have to jergle-er-juggle to earn a living now?"

Peroline nodded. "I 'ave the sack from Monsieur Bourgeois. I need the money for my study. I am a student in Paris."

"Do you like juggling?" Wanda asked.

"Yes, but I don't earn so much money." Peroline stood up ready to move on. "Poor Pierre. 'E has to stay at the campsite to work for this 'orrible man, Bourgeois. I feel so sorry!" They walked together up the golden sand dune towards the road, the sun still warm on their backs.

"Me too!" Wanda agreed.

Peroline stopped in her tracks and shook her head sadly. "But what is it that we can do? Nothing!"

Wanda looked up at Peroline's serious, oval face, her grey eyes, her golden hair – looking like a film star who needs to be rescued from the villain of the piece. She felt suddenly brave and gallant. "Don't worry," she said, pulling her shoulders back and squaring her jaw. "We'll think of something! We'll get your job back for you!"

She turned on her heels like a pony prancing off into the prairie. She waved at the fair Peroline and trotted off in a cloud of sand, brave and true, into the red sunset.

CHAPTER 9

That evening the Waymans and the Millers skipped the disco. It wouldn't be the same without Peroline. They sat quietly under their awnings, drank wine together, strolled down to the lake. After dark, even Mrs Wayman ventured out of the car and tried to pretend she was enjoying herself. Meanwhile, Wanda, Flora and Jim got out the bats and balls for a game of beach tennis on the grass. It was more fun to play in the dark with the luminous pink ball.

"Game, set and match to Miss Wayman!" Wanda shouted at an exhausted Jim after one hour of play. "Six two, six one, six love!"

"But *he* had the broken bat," Flora pointed out.

Wanda looked at her friend fiercely. "Whose side are you on?" she said.

Jim was gracious in defeat, then he swiftly beat her at Scrabble with 'xylophone' on a triple-word score. Wanda huffed until bedtime.

Next morning Mr Wayman was up with the lark. Wanda peered out of her compartment to see him brewing tea.

"Da-ad, what time is it?" she yawned.

"Six fifteen. Ssh!"

She crawled out of bed. "Dad, even the Dutch family opposite aren't up yet! What on earth are you doing!"

"Ssh. Just roll up your sleeping-bag and pack your gear. Get Flora to do the same!" He began putting jars of jam and tins of beans into a cardboard box. "Go on, Wanda, do as you're told."

"He's given in! Mum's persuaded him to pack up and go! We're leaving!" Wanda reported miserably to Flora. Flora, with tear-filled eyes, sat down to scribble a farewell message to Jim. Wanda hardly had the heart to tick off items on her list: T-shirts – 7, shorts – 5, etcetera.

"Look lively, you two!" Mr Wayman hissed. "Don't make a noise. Just help your mum sling some cases in the boot. Ready?"

With heavy hearts, Flora and Wanda were admitting defeat. Bourgeois had won. He had ruined their holiday.

"Right," said Mr Wayman. "The car's jam packed, so you two will have to walk." He was turning the ignition key. Mrs Wayman sat bolt upright in the passenger seat, trying not to see horseflies.

"Walk!" Wanda and Flora squeaked. The ferry port was miles away. Eighty-seven kilometres, to be exact.

Wanda's dad tutted at them. "Yes, walk. Just follow the car. It's not far. Ready?"

Wanda and Flora looked at each other and raised their eyebrows. The old tent was empty, the car was full. The sun was coming up through the branches of the pine tree. "Ready!" they said, with a thumbs-up sign. What on earth was Mr Wayman up to now?

At emplacement 53 the horseflies had begun to drop gently on to the flysheet to greet the new day. Flora silently delivered her note to Jim next door. She propped it on their white plastic table, then she ran to catch up with Wanda. They both followed the dusty, laden car ... down the row from their old tent, turn right towards the lake, past the shower block, over a small crossroads away from the trees, along the lakeside.

Wanda and Flora stared at one another. This wasn't the way to the main exit!

The breeze rippled the blue surface of the lake. Two swans looked idly at the girls as they trotted by. Finally, Mr Wayman pulled up beside a smart, clean, green and blue tent, neatly zipped, surrounded by flowering bushes, bright as a new pin, and not a pine tree in sight!

He leapt out of the car. "Action stations!" he said, flinging a couple of sleeping-bags at the girls. "Come on, chop, chop! Then we can all have breakfast."

In five minutes the new tent was unzipped, the contents of the Wayman foodbox were in the new fridge, the contents of their suitcases were hanging in the new bedrooms. Mrs Wayman unpacked her shampoos and creams and sprays with a broad smile on her face. She took a deep breath, stepped outside, scanned the new flysheet for intruders. Not one! "I'm off for a shower," she said. She strode across the grass, a new woman.

"Well!" Wanda looked in amazement at her dad, the hero.

"What will Mr Bourgeois say?" Flora murmured.

"Who cares?" Wanda was changing into her swimming costume. "My dad can stand up to him any day!" She felt very proud of the Waymans.

Mr Wayman gave them both a wink as he went to twiddle the car radio knob for news of the latest cricket score. "All right you two?" he asked.

Wanda nodded and looked up at a clear blue sky, looked down and saw it reflected in the lake. She breathed deeply. "You bet!" she said before they scampered down to the lakeside to paddle. It was one-nil to Wayman United!

CHAPTER 10

"Oh no!" Flora panicked, up to her knees in pondweed.

"What now?" Wanda had her nose down at water level, squinting at frogspawn.

Flora was remembering word for word the farewell note she had left for Jim on the Millers' breakfast table. "I'll never ever forget you. See you in my dreams ... always always remember ..." The sort of thing you only ever write if you never expect to see someone again. But Jim was just three hundred metres up the track, tucking into croissants and reading her note. Flora wanted to die of embarrassment. "Nothing," she said weakly to Wanda, who would never understand affairs of the heart. Flora's knees trembled, and she lost all interest in the reproductive methods of frogs.

It was mid-morning and Mrs Wayman was saying hello to their new neighbours, a French couple with a white poodle. Mr Wayman was quietly enjoying England's test match success against the West Indies when the bombshell dropped.

The bombshell was Monsieur Bourgeois. He exploded on them, firing angry words like shrapnel, waving his arms, beating his fists in the air, spitting like fury.

"Colin, I think this gentleman wants a word with you," Mrs Wayman said at her most charming and sweet.

Mr Wayman turned off his radio and emerged from the car into the fresh morning air. "Hello, Mr Bourgeois, it's a grand day," he said by way of greeting. "Now what can we do for you?"

Wanda and Flora were enjoying the show. Bourgeois pffed and pshawed and blew steam through his nose. His moustache seemed now to disappear inside the crevice between his nose and his lips, while his pot-belly shook like jelly. The French couple came to watch. The two Dutch cyclists from down the way paused with their sticks of bread. A groundsman rested on his mower. Even the Millers had come trotting down the track when they got wind of the Bourgeois explosion.

Wanda watched her dad go all innocent. "Look," he said, "we only used our common sense. We were in a dirty tent by the pine tree with giant flies all over it. Here was a clean tent out in the open with no flies, see? Empty. We moved, simple as that. Well, what would you have done?" He appealed to members of the audience. "I ask you!" His speech was greeted by a little spattering of applause.

Bourgeois fumed and shook. Jim sidled up to the girls and gave them an encouraging wink. He gave Flora a special grin which melted her knees. She sat on the grass for safety, Jim alongside her. Wanda went and stood shoulder to shoulder with her dad. She stared defiantly at the enemy.

"It is not allowed!" Bourgeois ranted in English at last. "I have not permitted it!" He looked round enraged. "You must go, now!" He made herding movements like shooing sheep. "Go! Away from this place. Now!" He made as if to go into their tent to help them pack.

Wanda held her breath. Mrs Wayman stood in the doorway and drew herself up to her full one and a half metres. "The worm has turned!" she said darkly.

Confused, Bourgeois backed off, straight into the much taller figure of Mr Wayman. "Now look, steady on!" Wanda's dad warned. "We've paid good money for this holiday!"

Bourgeois spun round, the colour of thunderclouds. "In Camping Paradiso it is not allowed to choose!" he yelled. "Out! I tell you, go!"

By now everyone was backing the Waymans. The Millers explained carefully to the French couple. More onlookers had gathered. They were all shaking their heads. The French couple went up and told Bourgeois it was a shame. Their dog snapped at his heels. Still the manager shouted. The two tall, silent Dutchmen stepped in. They handed over their bread to the Millers. Then they marched forward and grabbed Bourgeois, one elbow each. They lifted him off the ground and carried him legs kicking, back up the track. Bourgeois shouted, the crowd clapped, Wanda laughed.

All you could see were the manager's little legs kicking helplessly between the long legs of the Dutchmen. His voice faded in the distance. Peace returned.

Two-nil. Wanda chalked up another goal. Her mum was basking in the sunshine beside the flowering currants. Her dad was sipping a lager with their tall Dutch neighbours.

Wanda kept thinking of poor Peroline, kept out of the side completely. It was two-one really, and Wanda had the uneasy feeling that they had only reached half-time. There was still a long way to go.

She saw herself in an all-white strip cutting through the defence. She headed like lightning for goal. The crowd was roaring, the news photographers' bulbs were flashing, Bourgeois was face down in the mud, spreadeagled, defeated by her cracking shot!

"Oh Wanda!" Flora broke into her victory with a tearstained face. "Have you heard the news? It's terrible!"

"What now?" She grabbed Flora to make her sit down at the table under the awning.

"It's Jim and his family. It's that horrible Bourgeois!" Flora was in floods of tears. "He's making them leave the campsite!"

"How? What for?" Wanda couldn't believe it.

"He is! He can't get us because everyone's on our side, so he has to let us stay. But he hates Jim's family because they're our friends, so he's made up some horrible lie about them being too rowdy during the night. Honestly! And he's making them leave! He is, you've got to believe me! Jim's leaving! Oh!" Flora sobbed breathlessly all over her swimming towel.

"He can't do that," Wanda said, frowning.

"He can! He is!"

Wanda knew that he could really, and that it was true. She remembered the poor old American couple. "Stay here," she told Flora, and she sprinted up the hill to emplacement 54, just in time to see Mr Miller tighten the last rope on the roof rack, climb into the car and edge it up the main drive towards the gate. Jim, in the back seat, gave a sad little wave.

Wanda waved back. Bourgeois had got his revenge!

Chapter 11

Next morning a notice appeared in the office window. It was printed in French, English and German. Alongside a smiling mugshot of the odious Bourgeois ran a bold black headline: CAMPSITE MANAGER OF THE YEAR!

Wanda crushed her croissants in amazement. "What! Look at that!" She smashed the bag containing their breakfast against a nearby wall. "It must be a mistake!"

Flora edged nearer to the notice for a better view:

Azure Holidays are pleased to announce the winner of this year's Campsite Manager of the Year award. In the opinion of the judges, Monsieur Henri Bourgeois comes top of the class for friendliness and efficiency. Our supervisor praises his charming way with campers, especially the youngsters.

Camping Paradiso offers Azure service at its very best - all thanks to our Manager of the Year, Henri Bourgeois!

Jean Jacques Martin
(Managing Director)

P.S. Mr. Bourgeois will receive his award from the Managing Director of Azure Holidays tonight in person at the Seventies Disco.

Be There or Be Square!

It was the sensation of the day. People grumbled about it in the endless queue for bread, they chuntered about it in the showers, cold as usual. Children snorted and laughed about it outside the locked games room. Manager of the Year! "Doesn't say much for all the rest!" Wanda's dad commented, good-naturedly.

But Wanda was fuming. "How can he be the best? How do they know? Who did they ask? I bet they never asked a single camper!"

"It's that supervisor, Miss Thingummy!" Flora murmured. She was having a bad day; Jim had gone and the whole world seemed empty without him. She expected to meet up with his freckled face around every corner – and every minute she was disappointed all over again. She sighed and went to lie down in the tent, pretending that she had a stomach ache.

Worse still, Bourgeois did his morning moped rounds with a smug look on his face. His nose was in the air, he looked graciously to left and right, gave a little royal wave and rode on. "He looks different!" Wanda said to herself. She tracked him for a couple of minutes. "He definitely looks different!" She studied his slicked back black hair, his too-big nose. "That's it!" She saw what it was; he'd trimmed his moustache! Now it looked like a little black nailbrush perched at the end of his nose all even and bristly. "I'll bet it's to make a good impression tonight!" Wanda snorted, trekking back to base. "I wonder if they'll give him a medal, or what!"

Her mum was sunbathing happily beside the lake. "Cheer up, Wanda!" she said.

"I won't!" Wanda said glumly. Nothing anyone could say was worse than this instruction to cheer up when you were feeling down. She went in and dumped herself at the foot of Flora's bed. "Fancy a walk down the beach?" The worst thing of all was the helplessness. Wanda just wasn't used to it. It was no good being super-brainy, super-organised, super-anything against the likes of Bourgeois. In the end it was better to just keep out of his way.

The two girls took themselves off down the farm lane, past the rows of green lettuce, past the noisy grey geese. Wanda hissed back at them through the wire netting. "Well!" she challenged Flora.

They trudged the rest of the way with their heads down, nursing their bad moods like blisters on their feet. Even the sparkling blue sea beyond the biscuit-coloured sand dunes failed to excite them. Lemon and turquoise windsurfers sliced the waves. Little black dogs chased their tails in mad circles in the stifling heat. Children squealed at the white breakers. But still Wanda and Flora refused to be cheered up.

"Hey!" A voice yelled at them in the distance. "Hey, you two!"

Flora jumped as if she had been stung.

"Hey, Flora!" It was Jim's voice. It was Jim's legs and Jim's bright shorts ploughing through the sand. It was Jim's freckles and his sandy red hair.

Flora threw off despair like a raincoat when the sun comes out. She flung her arms around Jim's shoulders and they capered in the sand.

It was ages before she found the common sense to ask him what he was doing there.

"Helping Peroline," he said, pointing across the beach. "She's teaching me to juggle!"

There was Peroline juggling in the sun, surrounded by a crowd of tanned, colourful sunbathers.

"Yes, but what are you doing *here!*" Wanda repeated. "We thought you'd gone home because of Bourgeois."

"No!" Jim exclaimed. "We only had to move down the road. Fabulous campsite, right by the beach. Camping Sables D'Or; Golden Sands, see!"

They could see the rows of tents, the waterslide, everything.

"Great!" Flora beamed. The rest of her holiday fell into place again; beach romps, being a juggler's assistant, with Jim by her side!

"Yes, great!" Wanda agreed. Bourgeois hadn't beaten the Millers. She smiled. She even admitted to herself that she was a tiny bit glad to see Jim.

"Hi!" said Peroline, as the old trio tramped back across the sand to her pitch. "What's new?" She packed up her clubs for a lunch break. The crowd drifted off slowly.

"Bourgeois has been made Campsite Manager of the Year!" Wanda reported. "Did Pierre tell you?"

Peroline made a sour face and shook her head. "Now 'e must work all day, all night. 'E must do the job of two people."

"You never see him then?"

"Five minutes maybe." Peroline put on a brave smile.

"You want to share some bread and cheese?"

"Thanks." Wanda took some fresh bread. "Bourgeois gets his award tonight." She was getting lost in thought, staring at the shimmering horizon.

"Good then. I will come to say well done!" Peroline said in a flat, sarcastic voice.

"Yes, he gets this presentation some time during the disco, with everyone there watching." Wanda's attention had wandered so much that the cheese dropped off her bread into the sand. Her mouth fell open.

"Oh-oh, Wanda!" Flora warned. She could see an IDEA forming in her friend's brain. "Ignore her!" she mouthed to Jim and Peroline. Flora had seen it all before.

When Wanda had an IDEA she behaved in an unusual way. Like now. She jumped up. She threw her lunch in the air for a passing seagull.

"Ignore her!" Flora said again.

Wanda stamped the sand and pummelled her fists in the air like an American football player. She sprinted to the water's edge and ran into the waves, splashing and yelling. She came back drenched.

"I said, don't take any notice!" Flora insisted frantically. "She only does it for attention!" Jim stared.

Wanda flung her wet arms around Peroline. "You're a genius!" she beamed.

"I am?" Peroline looked doubtful. "Why? What did I do?"

"You gave me an IDEA!"

"What? What?" Jim demanded to know.

"Don't ask. She won't tell you!" was Flora's advice.

Wanda steamrollered on. "Peroline, you said you'd come along to the disco tonight! That's it! You come along; you and Jim! Come along to the Golden Manager of the Century Celebrations. And you just wait and see what happens!"

Wanda Wayman, Mistress of Mystery, hugged her bright secret. Then she turned ten excited cartwheels in the sand.

Chapter 12

Flora flew along the rows of tents at Campsite Paradiso. She carried a big banner. 'TONIGHT! SEVENTIES DISCO! BE THERE OR BE SQUARE!' She stopped every so often to persuade a bunch of reluctant kids to come along.

"I dunno. They're usually pretty boring," was the answer. "Especially if Bourgeois runs it himself."

"This one won't be. It's special," she promised.

"What, dressing up as a hippy?" they said, unconvinced. They scuffed their trainers against the tent pegs.

"Yes. Tell your mum and dad. It's going to be good!" Off she went, advertising Bourgeois' big event.

Mr and Mrs Wayman watched with interest. There was Flora with her banner, and over there by the lake was their very own Wanda, deep in conversation with Pierre. It was late afternoon, a deeply peaceful time of day.

"They're up to something!" Mr Wayman said, one eye closed. He was struggling to stay awake on his sunlounger. A glittering horror novel lay face down and unread on his hairy chest.

"As usual," Mrs Wayman agreed. Her lobster shoulders were turning to honey brown at last. She passed him the suncream for a top up. "And, Colin, remember your nose this time!"

Holiday paradise for parents! So the girls went about their mysterious business uninterrupted.

"Right?" Wanda said at last. She'd checked it through one last time with Pierre. He knew exactly what he had to do. "You're sure Bourgeois will follow the same routine as usual?" she insisted.

Pierre nodded. "Always exactly the same. I play the records and he mimes the words and sometimes he pretends to play the guitar." He looked down at Wanda. "You think this will work?" Why should he trust this little kid with his job, his romance, his whole future?

Wanda could see which way his mind was working. "Trust me, Pierre!" she said calmly and firmly. "Operation Disco is foolproof!"

So Pierre went off to meet up with Peroline and Jim at the gates of Camping Sables D'Or.

At 18.00 hours Flora returned to the tent and reported complete success. "Everyone's coming!" She flopped exhausted on her bed.

"Now for the fancy-dress costumes," Wanda thought. No time for her to take a breather.

She found two flowing summer skirts in her mum's suitcase, one with orange and black flowers and frills, one with silver stripes on a dark green background. She held them against her waist to check they were floor length and hippyish. With a belt to tighten the waist they would be perfect. A quick check with her mum that she could borrow them (not giving her time to say no), and

Wanda moved on. For their tops they could wear plain dark swimming costumes, on their feet nothing. They would wear their hair loose, draw coloured flower patterns on their cheeks with her mum's kohl pencils. Around their necks they would wear long silk scarves, beads and pendants, at least six of these each; bangles round the wrists. And, crowning glory, in their hair they would wear handfuls of white blossom from the bushes by their tent. Perfect!

By 19.30 hours Wanda and Flora were floating round with happy hippy smiles, practising saying, "Love and peace, man!" and taking tips from Mr Wayman. "You've got to hand out flowers to everyone you meet. I seem to remember that was what it was all about, this love and peace stuff." He got no help from Wanda's mum, who was pretending to be too young to know.

The disco began at 20.00 hours. All over the camp, music from the seventies blared out to announce the start. From every direction, kids in flowered skirts and shirts drifted towards the bar. Wanda checked final details for Operations Disco in her own head as she and Flora joined the colourful crowd.

Dusk had gathered in the trees behind the pool, and little clusters of families sat drinking quietly, waiting for the disco to start. The dance floor was empty There was still no sign of Bourgeois and his honoured guests. "Love and peace!" Wanda and Flora said to all their friends, handing out a flower, hiding a grin. Peace wasn't really on the cards tonight, not if they got their way.

But where was Bourgeois? People were shuffling about. They grew impatient. Pierre had already manned the sound deck at the far end of the room and he was changing the music on cue. But the little stage was still empty. Red and blue lights flashed in the dark hall, and tiny white sparks of light cascaded from a rotating silver globe overhead. There was no Peroline to bring the disco to life. Where was Bourgeois?

A lone figure swept across the empty dance floor towards the stage, but it couldn't be the site manager, could it? It was wearing a long purple robe covered in silver embroidery all down the front. Its stomach jutted out slightly under the flowers and curly patterns of the robe. It wore a long, straight black wig, parted down the middle and slightly askew. It had bare feet and looked as if it had stepped straight out of an ancient music video. Only the face gave it away. Wanda and Flora stared closely at the clipped, bristly black moustache. It was Bourgeois!

CHAPTER 13

There was a big gasp as everyone recognised the Manager of the Year. Several parents went outside to laugh in private. The kids laughed out loud, their mouths wide open.

Completely at ease, Monsieur Bourgeois took the microphone. He said everything three times, in French, English and German. "Welcome everyone to our Seventies Disco," he said. "And tonight we have a special welcome for two very important guests, Mademoiselle Valerie Popigneau, our area supervisor, and Monsieur Jean Jacques Martin, the managing director of Azure Holidays." Bourgeois sounded as if he were introducing the prime minister. He wore his very smug smile. There was polite applause.

Smooth Monsieur Martin stood up to take a bow. He wasn't in fancy dress, but the glamorous Miss Popigneau was. Wanda admired her pure white smock and flowery, flared trousers. She even had flowers in her silky hair. She had gone to a lot of trouble.

"And now, music!" Bourgeois declared, waving everyone on to the dance floor.

"Oh good!" thought Wanda, for the first time in her life.

A few unwilling dancers responded, while Bourgeois went over to be nice to his important guests.

"Oh dear!" Wanda felt a flicker of panic. Why wasn't he miming to the record, as Pierre had said he would? She checked round and she could see Jim and Peroline standing ready in the dark doorway. More people had come on to the dance floor. Her own dad was showing people how to wave their arms around to the floaty music. They were beginning to have a good time!

This wasn't meant to happen! Wanda sent Flora across to Pierre with a hasty secret message. She waited in position. The reply soon came: "Later," Flora reported. "He begins the mime later. Pierre says he always waits for 'Lucy in the Sky'."

"What's that?" Wanda hissed.

"A song. Don't panic. Pierre says you just have to wait!"

Wanda steeled her nerves, kept the enemy in sight, and bided her time. The plan was a daring one, even for Wanda. For instance, Operation Disco involved her having to dance in public!

When Bourgeois stood up from the VIP table and began to thread his way through the gyrating hippies towards the stage, Wanda took to the dance floor. She waved her arms and twirled with the best of them. All in the course of duty, she told herself grimly.

When Bourgeois mounted the platform, Wanda positioned herself in a snowstorm of whirling, coloured lights. Round and round she went, twirling to the music.

Then Bourgeois took the fake microphone and cleared his throat, for all the world as if he was going to burst into song. Wanda tilted nearer towards Pierre's sound-board.

At the exact moment when the aged hippy threw back his head and opened his mouth to wail 'Lucy in the Sky with Diamonds', Wanda whirled extra fast, lost her balance, crashed into Pierre, who wrenched a vital wire out of its socket!

Bourgeois opened his mouth to dead silence. Dancers froze like musical statues. Onlookers watched, open-mouthed. The manager opened his own mouth like a fish: "Lucy in the sky-y with di-amonds!" No sound except his own weedy, reedy unmusical voice. He froze, rolled his eyes wildly under his wig, and panicked. He couldn't move. He stood in the crashing silence, transfixed!

It was Mr Wayman's loud laughter that broke the spell. Wanda recognised it as she hugged Pierre in a dark corner of the hall – fingers, toes, everything crossed. "Oh, I say!" her dad roared, laughing from deep down in his belly. Then everyone joined in. Every single dancer on the floor and drinker at the bar fell about laughing at the ridiculous figure, wig askew, useless microphone in his hand, gaping and gasping like a stranded herring. He was the laughing stock of Camping Paradiso.

Mademoiselle Popigneau rose to her dainty feet with a little cry. Her Manager of the Year had gone the colour of cherry brandy. The campers hooted at him, pointed and rolled in the aisles. Her managing director was staring coldly at her. The axe was about to fall.

"Mademoiselle, you chose this ... this ... idiot for Azure Holidays' Manager of the Year?" he hissed at her through narrow lips.

The hall was in chaos. Monsieur Bourgeois in his purple caftan was still stranded on stage. The laughter grew like an uncontrollable genie, out of its lamp and on the rampage.

"So!" Monsieur Martin said to Mademoiselle Popigneau with terrifying self-control. "You will go. I will fix this mess!"

Wanda watched the super-supervisor dash to the Ladies. She smiled with undisguised delight as she watched the big boss of Azure Holidays stride across the hall. This was it! Bourgeois had had it! A public disgrace, he would be sacked. The campers would cheer as Jim brought the lovely Peroline back on stage to rescue the evening. All would be well!

The boss reached Bourgeois, who was now the colour of his caftan and spluttering wildly. Wanda grinned from ear to ear. But what was this? Monsieur Martin had seized Monsieur Bourgeois by the shoulders and was kissing him on both cheeks! He was shaking his hand!

The director faced the rioting audience and appealed for calm. "Brilliant! Superb!" he was saying in three languages. "We must all thank Henri Bourgeois for his splendid performance! He must go on the television! Never have I seen such a funny show!" He clapped loudly and pushed Bourgeois forward to take a bow.

The laughter died down. Someone coughed. Another

person clapped. Wanda felt dismay drain the blood from her cheeks. She drifted to the foot of the stage in disbelief. Monsieur Martin was drawing a parchment scroll from his inside pocket, he was clearing his throat. "And now, ladies and gentlemen, I wish to present this important award to our favourite disco comedian, our popular organiser and children's friend, and above all, our Manager of the Year: Henri Bourgeois." His voice rose to an enthusiastic yell. He led the applause as Bourgeois stepped forward and took the red sealed award. The bewildered campers joined in. Soon there was a storm of clapping throughout the hall.

Wanda looked wildly round the room. Peroline stood in the doorway, shaking her head. Pierre looked away at the wall, unable to bear it. Jim and Flora were holding hands in shock. The disco lights splashed the white walls and the faces of the fancy-dress dancers.

Monsieur Martin smiled and smoothly ordered more music. The dancing began again. Bourgeois escorted Martin back to his table. His own smile was set hard as concrete. He spotted Wanda on his way back to the stage and let out an uncontrollable snarl. Wanda jumped a mile.

Bourgeois was back on stage, the sound-board was back in working order. 'Lucy in the Sky' wailed over the heads of the dancers. He 'sang' his socks off up there, completely happy with the way things had turned out.

Wanda's shoulders sagged. The flowers in her hair drooped. Bourgeois had won again!

CHAPTER 14

But not so fast. This time Wanda had an emergency back-up plan in mind. Operation Disco was not yet complete.

She ushered Flora and Jim outside into the darkness.

Mr Wayman looked in bewilderment at his wife. "Search me," he said, turning back to watch the terrible, no-talent Bourgeois killing the evening stone dead yet again with his dreadful mimes. He droned on and on:

> "Lucy in the sky-y with di-amonds,
> Lucy in the sky-y with di-amonds,
> Aaah-aaah!"

Mademoiselle Popigneau had returned to Monsieur Martin's table and sat smiling nervously ... until a faint marching sound was heard. "Left, right, left!" It started quietly, out by the pool. It was Wanda's voice: "Left, right, left!" A crowd by the door split down the middle to let the marching column enter the hall. "Left, right!" Dancers fell to one side. Wanda led her two marchers to the middle of the floor, where the lights fell on to their giant white placards. "Halt!" Wanda yelled.

Flora, Jim and Wanda held their signs high in the air. Their message shouted out loud and clear in huge black letters on a white background:

Shocked silence greeted them. Pierre cut the sound system once more. Wanda, Flora and Jim turned on the spot – left, right – showing the messages slow and clear, like judges at a skating competition.

"Yeh!" said a lone kid's voice at the back of the room. "Ban Bourgeois!"

"Yeh! Bring back Peroline!" others agreed. Soon a huge gang of children, half in hippy gear, half out, all chanting "Ban Bourgeois! Bourgeois is a bully! Bring back Peroline!" and marching on the spot, filled the hall.

The manager went pale. His face looked green under the disco lights. Monsieur Martin sprang to his feet, but this time he couldn't rescue Bourgeois. Mr Wayman stepped across his path and began to explain the truth of things, very slowly and loudly in short, no-nonsense English words.

"Quick march!" Wanda yelled. She led her motley army up and down the dance floor chanting:

"What do we want?"

"The sack for Bourgeois!"

"When do we want it?"

"Now!"

"What do we want?"

"The sack for Bourgeois!"

Up and down the hall, up and down. Every single child (and some adults) joined in.

Then Bourgeois snapped. He waved his arms like a windmill, trying to mow down Wanda's crocodile of chanting children. Their shrill voices rose above his angry roar. He headed for the ringleader with her 'Ban Bourgeois' placard. Wanda spotted him, head down, charging!

She was a Spanish bullfighter in a sparkling, sequinned jacket. She was a magnificent toreador. Olé! She whipped the cardboard sign to one side, like a bullfighter's cape, arched her back, one hand on her hip. Bully Bourgeois charged. Olé! Bourgeois blundered on. Wanda the Magnificent stamped the dusty earth and waved him on again.

Bourgeois roared. He charged. Wanda sidestepped neatly, and the manager went crashing through the door out on to the tiled terrace.

Wanda disapproved of all blood sports, except this one! She goaded the mad manager out across the patio towards the unguarded pool. She balanced at the poolside, hovering like an eagle, holding out her placard. Bourgeois, blind with fury, charged!

There was a moment, caught in time, when everyone gasped. It was before Bourgeois crashed and splashed headlong. Wanda's memory froze him forever at the split second when he realised the end had come. His jaw fell wide in silent agony, his arms were flung high in surrender. But it was already too late. His balance had gone. His foot caught the ledge, he tripped, toppled past the nimble Wanda, face forward, and fell with an almighty splash!

The crowd cheered. A huge wave of laughter greeted Bourgeois as he surfaced. His walrus face spouted water, his hair was plastered over his eyes and his purple caftan ballooned wetly around him.

A grinning Jim and Flora took Wanda's hands and raised them skyhigh. With their backs to the water, they walked forward victorious into the throng of clapping, cheering, laughing campers.

Chapter 15

In the calm after the storm of applause, the managing director of Azure Holidays abandoned his half-drowned Manager of the Year. He turned his back on him gasping at the shallow end and he gave Valerie Popigneau such a look that she wilted like a flower sprayed with weedkiller. As far as Wanda knew, they never darkened Monsieur Martin's door again.

He nodded and listened patiently to the campers. Yes, he understood. Bourgeois had lied and cheated his way through the summer season. He was very sorry. He, Jean Jacques Martin of Azure Holidays, was a reasonable man; what could he do to make up for it?

Wanda stepped right in with the perfect solution. She came within centimetres of the great man in his silky designer suit and expensive Italian shoes. Now was not the time to hesitate.

"Excuse me," she said, clearing her throat.

Monsieur Martin looked down. Here was a small child with flower petals in her hair, a crumpled T-shirt and a very determined look. "Yes, leetle girl?"

"We want you to bring back Peroline. She's brilliant. And she can juggle! We think you should make Pierre and Peroline joint managers of the camp, and give them a pay rise!"

"You do!" Monsieur Martin paled a little under his designer tan at the mention of a pay rise.

"Yes!" everyone agreed, pushing the blushing pair forward. Pierre and Peroline stood awkwardly awaiting the verdict.

Monsieur Martin looked down at Wanda. Sometimes appearances were not what they seemed. After all, she looked like a mousy English schoolgirl with spindly legs. But she was cunning, this little girl – and brave. "A pay rise?" he repeated slowly.

"Yes, so they can afford to go and study in Paris!" Wanda turned on her most enchanting smile. A sea of nodding faces backed her. A holiday evening smell of pizza, chips and aftersun lotion wafted in the warm breeze by the pool. Wanda hypnotised him with her powerful stare.

"Very well," Monsieur Martin agreed. "Peroline shall return. They will become the managers of this beautiful campsite, the jewel in the crown of Azure 'Olidays!" He backed off, half-smiling, shaking his head at the Amazing Wanda.

The crowd cheered again. Everyone hugged one another. Jim and Flora had to be prised apart. Even Mrs Wayman, not given to public displays of emotion, hugged her daughter. "Wanda, I'm proud of you!" she said.

Mr Wayman drank his daughter's health at the bar, joined by all the relieved parents. "She did a good job, your girl," they told him. "Getting rid of old misery guts. Maybe now we'll get some peace!"

Morning came. The sun rose in an azure blue sky. Even the dawn chorus sounded relieved. No more Bourgeois. No more bull.

"Hey look!" Flora poked her head out of the tent and rubbed her eyes. "Wanda, look!"

The Millers were back on site, unloading their gear into a tent down the row. Jim winked at them and gave a thumbs-up. Flora drowned in blushes.

"Great!" Wanda said, truly pleased that their old ally was back. She thumbs-upped in reply.

"Hey!" Jim said, splendid in his new, even brighter lime green swimming shorts. "Do you two know if we're still banned from the slide? What d'you reckon?"

Wanda and Flora were changed and ready to go in seconds. "Let's go and find out!" Wanda said.

The games room door was wide open, the crazy golf was already in full swing. Nothing was locked on this new day.

"Hi!" Wanda, Flora and Jim burst into the office, all smiles.

"'Ello!" Pierre and Peroline greeted them like sisters and brother; kisses on both cheeks, huge grins. "And 'ow are you?"

"Fine, fine!" They glanced sideways at each other. "Er, we wondered ... " they said in chorus, then giggled. "That is, we thought ... "

"Ah!" Peroline put up a finger to stop them, looked serious, then turned to speak with Pierre. Solemnly she turned back and stood them in a row, shoulder to shoulder. "And now," she announced, "the managers of Camping Paradiso wish to present an important award to Mademoiselles Wanda and Flora and Monsieur Jim."

The three of them stood there with held breaths, like Olympic athletes at a medal ceremony. Peroline, hiding a smile, said something to Pierre. "We wish to give you a thing which is very special. We wish to thank you." Her grin spread like sunshine. She dropped her act. "It is this," she said. She showered them with pink, blue, mauve, yellow and green waterslide tokens. Dozens of them. Hundreds of them.

"Free!" Pierre said.

"Free!" they squeaked. It was unbelievable, a dream come true.

"And free crazy golf. Free boating on the lake. Free pizzas!" Peroline was laughing and hugging them again. "We want to say thank you many many times!"

The three of them staggered delirious into the sunshine. They sprinted for the swimming pool. They scampered up the metal stairway to the top of the slide. They flung themselves, whooping and yelling and shouting down the snaky blue tube. Water whooshed around them. They took the bends at top speed. Water in their faces, water down their swimming costumes, water to greet them with a huge splash at the bottom.

All morning they dripped, climbed, slid and splashed. The sky grew bluer – the hot sun and the cool blue water. Wanda gazed down at the campsite from the full height of the waterslide. The tents were neat green and blue